PJMASKS

3-MINUTE BEDTIME STORIES

SIMON SPOTLIGHT

New York London Toronto Sydney New Delhi

SIMON SPOTLIGHT

An imprint of Simon & Schuster Children's Publishing Division
1230 Avenue of the Americas, New York, New York 10020

This Simon Spotlight edition August 2020

For information about special discounts for bulk purchases,
please contact Simon & Schuster Special Sales
at 1-866-506-1949 or business@simonandschuster.com.

Manufactured in China 0620 WGL

2 4 6 8 10 9 7 5 3 1

ISBN 978-1-5344-7057-6

ISBN 978-1-5344-7058-3 (eBook)

These titles were previously published individually
by Simon Spotlight with slightly different text and art.

Contents

It's Time to Save the Day!

What time is the right time for the PJ Masks to fight crime? Nighttime! That is because during the day, Amaya, Connor, and Greg go to school.

Today their class is trying to make the world's biggest omelette . . . when the eggs disappear!

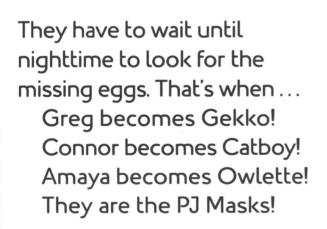

They have to wait until
nighttime to look for the
missing eggs. That's when . . .
Greg becomes Gekko!
Connor becomes Catboy!
Amaya becomes Owlette!
They are the PJ Masks!

Now it's time for the PJ Masks to fight crime! They find out that Romeo is using his Rotten-Ator to make all the eggs rotten—including a dinosaur egg that he took from the museum! Then Romeo starts throwing the rotten eggs at the PJ Masks!

The PJ Masks have a plan. Catboy makes the rotten eggs fresh again by turning the dial on the Rotten-Ator backward. He and the PJ Masks save the dinosaur egg too!

Another day, Amaya and Connor are eating lunch when Greg shows them a picture of a toy car he borrowed from a friend! Then the toy car vanishes!

That night, the PJ Masks find out that Luna Girl turned the toy car into her very own vehicle, so they take her Luna Board for a ride. Luna Girl wants her Luna Board back, so she agrees to trade it for the toy car!

After school another day, Amaya is playing soccer when she kicks the ball into a tree.
She goes to get her ball back, but she can't find it!

Luna Girl is hiding the soccer ball and other toys inside a giant moon ball!

That night, when the PJ Masks try to save the toys, Owlette gets stuck inside the moon ball too! The friends work together to pull the moon ball away from Luna Girl's strong Luna Magnet. Soon Owlette is safe—and so are the toys!

Now it's bedtime for Amaya, Connor, and Greg, but bedtime isn't just about pajamas for the PJ Masks. . . .

It's time to be a hero!

To the Cat-Car!

I'm **Catboy**, and this is the Cat-Car! It helps Owlette, Gekko, and me save the day! The Cat-Car has lots of special powers, just like I do.

Do you want to see the Cat-Car in action? We have to press the cat amulet in the center of the PJ Picture Player.

Now fasten your seat belt, and let's go!
PJ Masks, we're on our way! Into the night to save the day!

One of the Cat-Car's powers is the cat-roar! It makes a superloud noise. The cat-roar is perfect for deactivating Romeo's robots.

The Cat-Car is also superfast, just like me. When Luna Girl stole our friend Cameron's car, we needed Super Cat Speed to catch her.

And when Romeo created a machine that made things float, Gekko used the Cat-Car's special Cat-A-Pult jumping power to help Owlette get back on the ground. The PJ Masks saved the day!

Tonight, Night Ninja is causing trouble in the city. Let's use the Cat-Car's furballs to scare him off.

Uh-oh! He dodged the furballs! Night Ninja's Ninjalinos use Sticky Splats to stop the Cat-Car in its tracks.

While we're distracted, Night Ninja tries to steal the Cat-Car! But Night Ninja doesn't know how to drive, and he accidentally presses the seat-eject button. "You PJ Masks always ruin my plans!" Night Ninja says as he lands using his parachute.

PJ Masks all shout hooray!
'Cause in the night, we saved the day!
All thanks to the Cat-Car.

Fly High, Owl Glider!

Hi, I'm Owlette. And this is the Owl Glider! It helps Catboy, Gekko, and me save the day! The Owl Glider has some truly cool powers, just like me.

Do you want to see the Owl Glider fly into the night? First we have to press the owl amulet in the center of the PJ Picture Player.

Are you ready for a thrilling adventure? Buckle your seat belt and get ready to fly high with Catboy, Gekko, and me, Owlette! **PJ Masks, we're on our way! Into the night to save the day!**

Like me, the Owl Glider can see far into the dark night. Its high beams help us track down missing objects, like the golden microphone Luna Girl stole before a big concert.

Fluttering feathers! When Night Ninja took planes meant for an air show, all we needed was some Owl Glider turbo power to soar ahead and catch up to him and the Ninjalinos!

And when Night Ninja challenged the PJ Masks to a game of capture the flag, the Owl Glider's claws lent a big hand. The claws set Gekko down on the top of the school, where he captured all the flags!

Tonight Luna Girl is digging up trouble in the city gardens! She's planting special seeds and is using her nighttime Luna beams to make her moonflowers grow. Before long they will cover every inch of the city!

The Owl Glider's claws can pull up Luna Girl's wicked weeds—except Luna Girl keeps feeding them. They grow stronger and trap the Owl Glider's claws in their sticky branches! Luckily, teamwork helps the glider get unstuck.

Luna Girl underestimates us again. High above, the Owl Glider's powerful wings create a whirlwind that gathers the moonflowers' scattered seeds. We collect the weeds and toss them in the garbage where they belong!

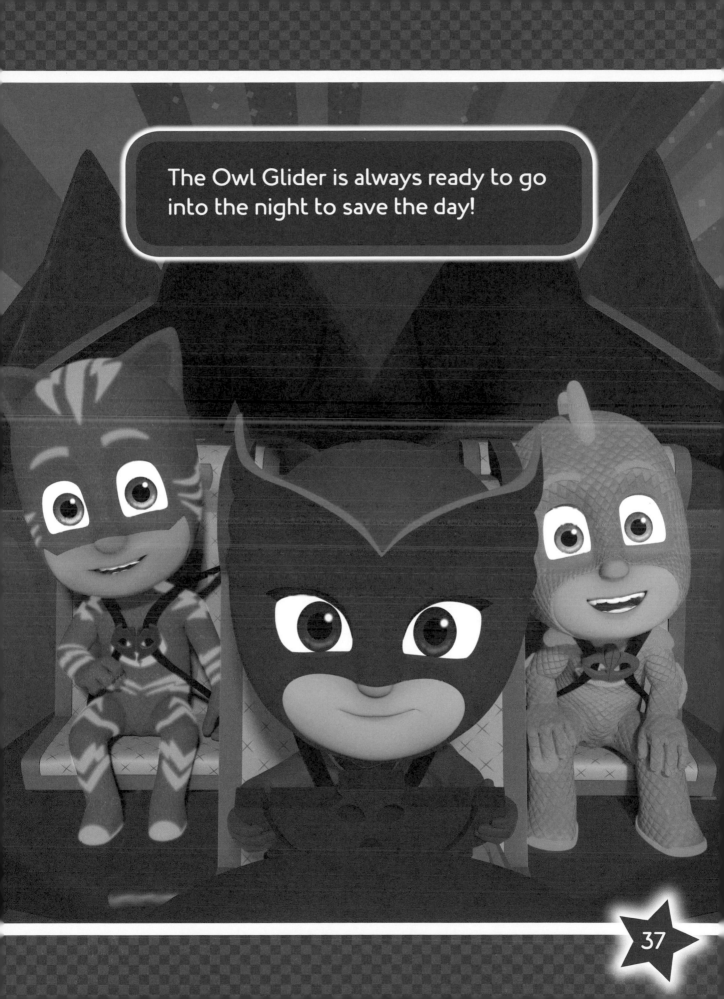

The Owl Glider is always ready to go into the night to save the day!

Go, Go, Gekko-Mobile!

Hi! I'm Gekko! And this is the Gekko-Mobile! It helps Catboy, Owlette, and me save the day! The Gekko-Mobile has tons of special powers, just like me.

Do you want to see the Gekko-Mobile go, go, go into the night? First we have to press the gekko amulet in the center of the PJ Picture Player.

Now buckle up your seat belt and get ready to dive deep into an exciting adventure with Catboy, Owlette, and me, Gekko! **PJ Masks, we're on our way! Into the night to save the day!**

Wriggling reptiles! The Gekko-Mobile isn't afraid of a little water. In fact, it travels above ground or below water.

The Gekko-Mobile can climb up anything, including the sides of buildings! Super Gekko Grip gives it a perfect power for chasing Luna Girl when she tries to get away!

And Super Gekko Camouflage helps us hide in plain sight. It was just the power we needed when Romeo unleashed a steady stream of spoiled, smelly eggs.

Night Ninja always has his eyes on the Gekko-Mobile. Once he and the Ninjalinos tried to steal it. But Night Ninja didn't understand the Gekko-Mobile's super strong powers and ended up losing control!

Another time, he challenged us to capture the flag with our headquarters as the prize. Night Ninja unleashed his Sticky Splats and trapped the Gekko-Mobile. We worked together and freed the Gekko-Mobile!

And when Night Ninja wanted his art to be the best in the world, he splattered paint on everyone else's artwork. But we tracked him down with the help of the Gekko-Mobile.

It's always time to be a hero . . . especially when the Gekko-Mobile is on your side!

Spring into Action!

Amaya, Connor, and Greg are growing sunflowers at school.

Connor and Greg offer to help Amaya with her flower, but Amaya says no. She thinks she is a gardening natural and doesn't need any help.

Amaya opens the gardening tool shed. But all the tools are gone!

It's time for the PJ Masks to spring into action!

Greg becomes Gekko!

Amaya becomes Owlette!

Connor becomes Catboy!

The PJ Masks find the missing tools in the park. They also find Luna Girl and a giant moonflower! "Just wait until this flower releases hundreds of seeds," Luna Girl says. "Soon there will be so many moonflower weeds that there won't be room for any other flowers!"

The PJ Masks gasp! They must stop Luna Girl before her moonflower weeds cover the entire city!

Owlette wants to dig out the flower, but Catboy and Gekko are worried.

"Big weeds have big roots," they say. "If even one root is left, it'll grow into another moonflower."

But Owlette doesn't listen to them.

Owlette tries to dig out the moonflower, but then she gets tangled in a branch!
Gekko uses his Super Gekko Muscles to untangle Owlette.

Owlette tries digging again, but Luna Girl gets in the way.

Then the moonflower blooms, releasing hundreds of seeds into the sky. More moonflowers start growing everywhere!

Owlette is sorry that she ignored her friends. She realizes she should have asked her friends for help instead of trying to solve this alone.

"I have another idea," Owlette says. "But I'm going to need all the gardening help I can get." Gekko and Catboy smile. The PJ Masks are now working as a team!

Gekko shines the Owl Glider's beams at the moonflowers. Owlette waters them. Normal plants like light and water. But since the moonflower is an evil weed, it shrinks and dies!

Next Owlette uses her Super Owl Wings to create a wind funnel. All the moonflower seeds in the sky fall into Catboy's bucket.

"You pesky PJ pests!" Luna Girl says as she flies away.

The PJ Masks have saved the day, thanks to their gardening skills and teamwork!

At school Amaya wins the prize for the best sunflower.

Amaya is thankful for Connor and Greg's gardening advice. "This is your trophy too," she says to her friends.

Whether they are growing flowers or saving the day, the PJ Masks work best as a team!

Race to the Moon!

Amaya, Greg, and Connor are learning about the moon. When the moon looks orange, it is called a harvest moon.

There will be a harvest moon tonight, and Luna Girl will be up to no good. This is a job for the PJ Masks!

Greg becomes Gekko!

Connor becomes Catboy!

Amaya becomes Owlette!

They are the PJ Masks!

The harvest moon makes Luna Girl's Luna Magnet stronger. She will use it to travel to the moon and find the harvest moon crystal. "The crystal will make my powers unstoppable!" says Luna Girl.

The PJ Masks will follow her. With PJ Robot's help, they transform Headquarters into a rocket ship. PJ Masks are on their way into space to save the day!

Luna Girl throws energy bubbles at the heroes' ship. Owlette manages to land the ship on the moon, but it needs to be repaired.

Gekko is worried. Being away from home makes him nervous. So does being in space. He stays on the ship with PJ Robot.

Catboy and Owlette race out on their PJ Rovers to stop Luna Girl.

67

They are too late. Luna Girl finds the harvest moon crystal and starts using its power.

The PJ Masks must stop her. Catboy tries to use his Super Cat Speed, but it doesn't work on the moon!

Luna Girl uses the harvest
moon crystal to capture
Owlette and Catboy.

Gekko watches the console in the rocket ship. He sees what Luna Girl is doing.

He hops on his PJ Rover and goes to help his friends.

Gekko uses his Super Gekko Muscles, and the heroes break free from the trap!

They work together to get the harvest moon crystal away from Luna Girl.

The PJ Masks saved the moon and stopped Luna Girl!

Super Cat Speed!

The school concert is tomorrow, but the instruments are missing! This is a job for the PJ Masks!

Amaya becomes Owlette!

Connor becomes Catboy!

Greg becomes Gekko!

They are the PJ Masks!

The PJ Masks hear a loud noise.

It's Night Ninja! He is singing while the Ninjalinos play the missing instruments. They are his backup band.

Catboy will use his Super Cat Leap to trap the Ninjalinos, but he hesitates and it does not work.

Owlette is sad. If they can't return the instruments, then there won't be a concert.

Catboy does not like to see his friend sad. He uses Super Cat Speed!

He speeds around the Ninjalinos and takes back a recorder!

Catboy is afraid to play the recorder in front of everyone at the school concert. He's even afraid to play in front of his friends and the Ninjalinos, but he gives it a try.

Catboy is so good that the Ninjalinos do not want to be Night Ninja's backup band anymore. They want to play with Catboy!

An angry Night Ninja bangs the drum so hard that it flies up in the air and crashes down on him. He is stuck inside the drum.

The Ninjalinos return the instruments to the PJ Masks. Night Ninja is defeated again.

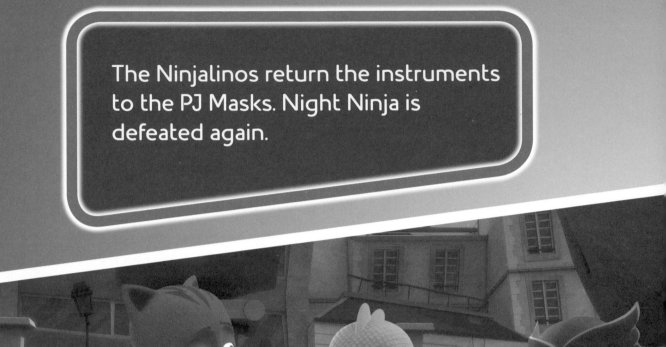

The PJ Masks save the day.
Hooray for the PJ Masks!

And hooray for Connor, who learns it is okay to be afraid as long as you try your best.

Hero School

Greg, Connor, and Amaya are leaving school. Oh no! The school bus is missing! This looks like a job for the PJ Masks!

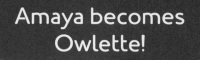

Amaya becomes Owlette!

Connor becomes Catboy!

Greg becomes Gekko!

They are the PJ Masks!

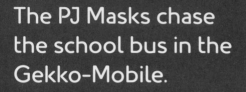

The PJ Masks chase the school bus in the Gekko-Mobile.

The Gekko-Mobile is too slow and the bus gets away!

Owlette and Catboy use their powers to find the bus. Night Ninja took it! Gekko runs off alone to stop him.

Night Ninja and the Ninjalinos are painting the bus blue. Gekko wants them to return it.

"No! The bus will be my super-car!" Night Ninja says. Night Ninja throws Sticky Splats at Gekko!

Owlette and Catboy arrive to help.

Gekko does not want help. He wants to be the hero all by himself.

Night Ninja throws
Sticky Splats at Catboy.

Owlette gets tangled
in her wings.

Gekko uses his Super Gekko Muscles to grab the bus.

While Gekko is distracted, Night Ninja steals the Gekko-Mobile!

Gekko calls for help. Owlette gets free and helps Catboy. Then they help Gekko. Together, the three heroes take the Gekko-Mobile back from Night Ninja!

"When we help each other, we cannot be beat!" says Gekko.

The heroes return the bus to school!

Gekko learned that even heroes need help sometimes. Hooray for the PJ Masks!

Catboy Saves the Sunshine

It is a beautiful summer day, and Connor, Greg, and Amaya are playing outside with their friends.

Suddenly, dark clouds fill the sky. It is so cold and gloomy that no one can play outside anymore!

Amaya sees a Luna Moth fly by. "This is Luna Girl's fault!" she gasps.

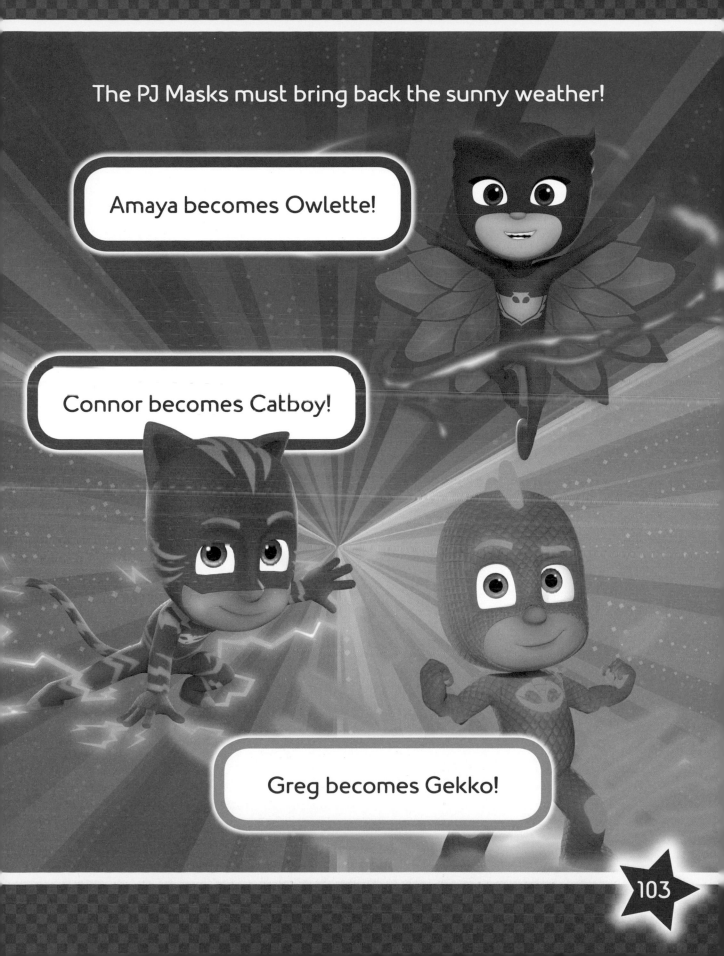

The PJ Masks must bring back the sunny weather!

Amaya becomes Owlette!

Connor becomes Catboy!

Greg becomes Gekko!

103

Luna Girl is using her Luna Magnet to make dark, stormy clouds.

"I never get to play summer games," Luna Girl says. "So I'm going to block out the sun with my clouds, and no one can play games!"

Catboy tries to use his Super Cat Speed to steal the Luna Magnet. But then Luna Girl creates a large rain cloud over Catboy's head, and it starts to pour!

"Aaah! I hate getting wet!" Catboy cries. Every time he tries to move, the cloud follows him.

Meanwhile, Luna Girl creates big gray clouds around Gekko and Owlette. They are trapped and can't see anything!

Catboy doesn't know what to do. He wants to save his friends, but if he moves, he'll get wet!

Catboy takes a deep breath. "I hate getting wet, but not as much as I hate letting my friends down. *Super Cat Speed!*" He runs toward Luna Girl, bringing the rain cloud along with him.

Now Luna Girl is soaked too!
   While she is distracted, Catboy grabs the Luna Magnet from her hand and points it toward the cloud. All the clouds disappear into the Luna Magnet.

"You did it, Catboy! You saved the sunshine!" Gekko says.

Catboy smiles. Getting wet isn't so bad if it means saving his friends.

PJ Masks all shout hooray! 'Cause in the night we saved the day!

Fly High, Owlette!

Today is the Loop-de-Loop air show. Connor and Greg tag along with Amaya, who is excited to see the planes soar through the sky just like her!

But when they arrive at the show, the planes are missing. "Look, footprints from Ninjalinos!" Connor says.

This is a job for the PJ Masks!

Connor becomes Catboy!

Greg becomes Gekko!

Amaya becomes Owlette!

They are the PJ Masks!

The PJ Masks use the Owl Glider to find Night Ninja. Night Ninja and the Ninjalinos are flying the stolen planes through the sky.

"I'll dazzle them with the Owl Glider's beams and make them land," Owlette says. "They've got no chance against a fantastic flyer like me!"

Night Ninja and the Ninjalinos fly into a formation and release Splat-Grabbers. They stick onto the Owl Glider's wings.

"I can't fly anywhere!" Owlette cries.

The Owl Glider crash-lands, and Night Ninja disappears into the sky!

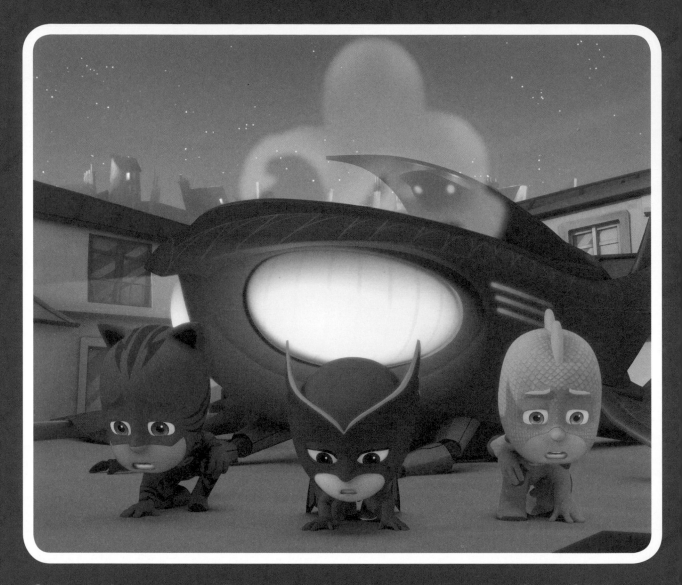

Catboy has a plan. First, they'll take the broken Owl Glider back to HQ. Then, Gekko and Catboy will borrow an old plane from the museum to chase after Night Ninja. Owlette will use her Owl Wings to lead the way.

Owlette doesn't want to lead. She thinks she's a bad flyer because she crashed the Owl Glider.

When the PJ Masks find Night Ninja again, he is trying to pull down HQ with his Splat-Grabbers. "I'll destroy HQ and the Owl Glider for good!" Night Ninja says with a cackle.

Catboy and Gekko turn to Owlette for a plan. But Owlette still thinks Night Ninja is a better flyer than her.

"You're an amazing flyer, Owlette!" Gekko says.

"Yeah, you're the only one who can stop Night Ninja!" Catboy agrees.

Owlette realizes that her friends are right. "Night Ninja may have out-flown me before, but now it's time to be a hero!" she says.

Thanks to Owlette's flying skills, the PJ Masks save HQ, the Owl Glider, and the Loop-de-Loop show planes!

"I'll catch you next time, PJ pests!" Night Ninja says.

PJ Masks all shout hooray! 'Cause in the night we saved the day!

Gekko Speaks Up

Greg, Connor, and Amaya are at school. Greg is nervous because he is reciting a poem in front of the class tomorrow. "Don't worry, you'll do great," Amaya and Connor say. But Greg gets really nervous reading in front of people! Suddenly, Greg gets zapped by a red glow from a mysterious box. He tries to speak, but his voice is gone!

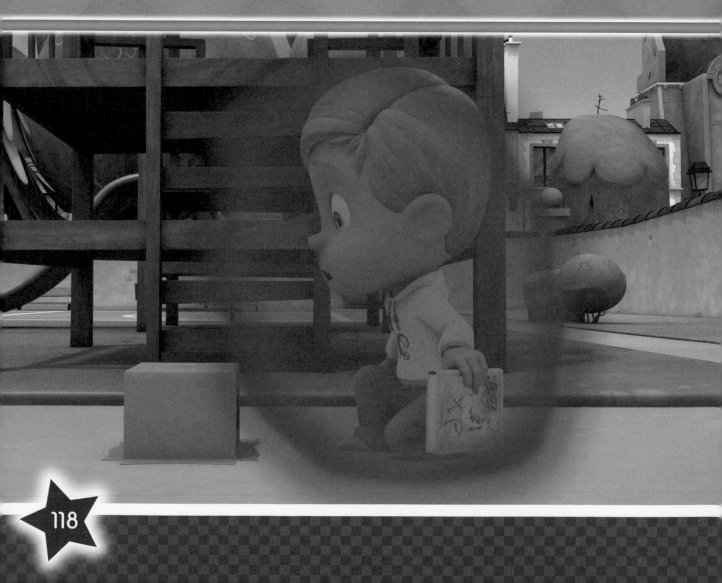

The PJ Masks must find out who stole Greg's voice!

Amaya becomes Owlette!

Connor becomes Catboy!

Greg becomes Gekko!

They are the PJ Masks!

The PJ Masks race into the night.

"You're my hero, Romeo!" Gekko suddenly shouts. Owlette and Catboy gasp, but Gekko shakes his head. He wasn't the one who spoke!

It was Romeo who stole Gekko's voice and is using it to play tricks!

Owlette and Catboy distract Romeo while Gekko finds the voice box. But then Gekko realizes that if he never gets his voice back, he never has to recite a poem. Gekko decides to leave the voice box where it is.

Zap! Zap! Now Catboy's and Owlette's voices are gone, too!
Romeo laughs in delight. "Imagine all the naughty things I
can do with these voices. And the PJ Masks will get the blame!"

Gekko is horrified. He didn't take the voice box when he could have, and now it's his fault that his friends have lost their voices.

Gekko can't let his fear of reading aloud get in the way anymore. "It's time to be a hero!" he mouths.

Gekko uses his Super Gekko Camouflage to sneak up behind Romeo. He snatches the voice box and presses the buttons.
    Zap! Zap! Zap!

"I can talk again!" Catboy says.

"I've got my voice back too!" Owlette says.

"And I've got mine!" Gekko says.

Gekko isn't so scared of reading a poem out loud anymore. After all, nothing is scary when his best friends are by his side!

PJ Masks all shout hooray! 'Cause in the night we saved the day!

PJ Masks Save the Library!

Amaya is excited to read her
Flossy Flash superhero book at storytime.

Oh no! Someone erased all the stories in the library! The books just have pictures of Romeo inside!

This looks like a job for the PJ Masks!

Greg becomes Gekko!

Connor becomes Catboy!

Amaya becomes Owlette!

They are the PJ Masks!

The PJ Masks look for Romeo. Catboy asks Owlette to use her Owl Eyes, but she wants powers like Flossy Flash instead.

Catboy hears Romeo with his Super Cat Ears.

Romeo has ruined more books!

The heroes make a plan to stop Romeo. But then Owlette pretends to be Flossy Flash and forgets to look for Romeo!

Romeo ties up Gekko and Catboy!

Owlette tries to help her friends by doing a Flossy Flash Flip, but she trips and falls!

Romeo laughs and steals more library books!

Owlette decides it's time to be her own hero. She sets Catboy and Gekko free.

Owlette uses her Owl Eyes and Super Owl Wings to look for Romeo.

She sees Romeo and distracts
him with her Flossy Flash book!
Romeo and his robot chase her.
They want every last book!

Meanwhile, Catboy and Gekko
set a trap for Romeo's robot. He
falls right into it and gets tangled
up in some rope.

Romeo can't go through with his plan!

The PJ Masks fix all the books and save the library! Hooray!